Darcy Brewster here,
reporting for duty.

I'm lucky I'm still around to tell my story.
It might have been very different
if I hadn't had the right stuffing.

BEAR

QUICK-DRAW McPAW

FURRY EAGLE

SIR EDWARD
THE IMPALER

ONE TRUE BEAR

Ted Dewan

Walker & Company   New York

Years ago, I was a young cub serving in the Bear Force. We were having trouble with a little boy named Damian.

Bear after bear was sent away to Damian's house on an important mission: to become his One True Bear.

But even the toughest and
bravest bears couldn't capture
Damian's heart or imagination.
He demolished them all.
They just didn't have
the right stuffing . . .

. . . and the Bear
Force was
quickly running
out of heroes.

One morning, our captain said to us,
"I'm sure you all know about Damian.
All our toughest bears have come
to grief trying to become
his One True Bear.

So this time I need a bear with
something truly special—I need
a bear with the right stuffing.
Any volunteers?"

I thought for a moment. Then I said,
"Yes, sir . . . I'm your bear."
"Darcy Brewster," said Captain,
"you are one very brave and good cub."

At sunrise the next day,
Captain said to me,
"Good luck, Darcy.
We'll watch over you."
"Thank you, sir," I said.

And I floated away from
Bear Force Headquarters,
never to return again.

When I landed at Damian's house, he picked me up and looked me in the eye.

For a moment, I thought it would all be okay.

But things soon got noisy.

And then things
got rough.

But I didn't cry.
I didn't fight back.
I looked him in
the eye and said . . .

"Please . . . don't pull off my arms.

I need my arms to hug you.
If you pull off my arms, how
will I hold you at night and
keep the bad dreams away?"

So he stopped.

And I lived to see another day.

On the second day, we were playing
a game, and my stuffing spilled out.

But I didn't cry.
I didn't fight back.
I looked him in the eye and said,
"Please . . . don't take out
my stuffing. I need my stuffing
to love you with all my heart.
Without it, how will I love you
when you are sad inside?"

So he patched
up my tummy . . .

and we played
a different game.

And I lived to see another day.

On the third day, we went
up a tree, but Damian left me
there until bedtime.

"Please don't leave me out here
in the cold, damp night.
I need my fur to comfort you.
If my fur is damp
and soggy, how will
I comfort you
when you're scared
of the dark?"

So I looked at him through
his window and said,

So he came to rescue
me from the tree . . .

and dried me off . . .

and we went on to
share another day.

And the day
after that.

And after a while . . .

it became clear something
had changed.

I had become . . .

... Damian's One True Bear.

The Happy Prince

It turned out I had the
right stuffing after all.

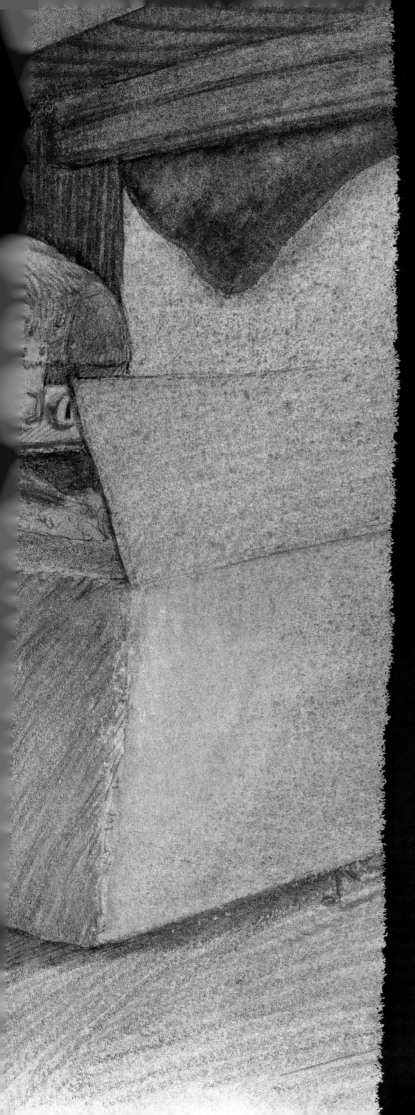

But then one day I fell under
the bed. I stayed there all day
and all night, waiting for
Damian to find me.

I waited all the next day.
I stayed there for months.
For years.
Just waiting.

Then, one stormy night,
someone came rushing into
the bedroom, pulling open
drawers and cupboards and
looking under the bed,
where finally he saw me.

He picked me up, dusted
me off, looked me in the eye,
and smiled.

It was **Damian**, all grown up
and dressed in a rescue uniform.
He needed me to go with him into the
storm on the toughest mission of all
and say good-bye to him forever.

I didn't cry.

I didn't fight back.

Because after all those many, many years,
tonight I finally knew for sure . . .

. . . Damian had the
right stuffing too.

To Pandora,
the greatest
adventure

To Heather,
for sharing the
dream

And to Joel,
for his
courage

Special thanks to the children who contributed drawings:
Keno Burckhardt, Anastasia Bartsch, Pandora Dewan, Alfie Haddon, Greg Holyoke, Clara Osmond Kantor,
Julia Monteiro, Laurence Mounce, Arthur Potts, Georgia Richardson, Jamie Selway, Leo Selway,
Patrick Selway, Theo Tarrega, Desi Tomaselli, Bryony Williams, Haley Wood

First published in Great Britain in 2009 by Orchard Books, a division of Hachette Children's Books
First published in the United States of America in 2009 by Walker Publishing Company, Inc.
Visit Walker & Company's Web site at www.walkeryoungreaders.com

For information about permission to reproduce selections from this book, write to
Permissions, Walker & Company, 175 Fifth Avenue, New York, New York 10010

Library of Congress Cataloging-in-Publication Data
Dewan, Ted.
One true bear / Ted Dewan.
p.   cm.
Summary: A brave teddy bear puts his fur on the line when he goes to live with a boy who has a long history of destroying his toys.
ISBN-13: 978-0-8027-8495-7 • ISBN-10: 0-8027-8495-X (hardcover)
[1. Teddy bears—Fiction. 2. Heroes—Fiction.] I. Title.
PZ7.D521125On 2009   [E]—dc22   2009001807

Printed in China by South China Printing Co. Ltd.
2 4 6 8 10 9 7 5 3 1

All papers used by Walker & Company are natural, recyclable products made from wood grown in well-managed forests.
The manufacturing processes conform to the environmental regulations of the country of origin.